THE UNEXPECTED

A HEARTBREAKING LOVE STORY

GOURI SHARMA

Made with ❤ on the Notion Press Platform
www.notionpress.com

A boy that I'm seriously, deeply, madly, incredibly,

and undeniably in love with..

And he taught me the most important thing of all ----

"Life is a game

and sarcasm is a cheat code.. "

You're remembered always and missed more.

Contents

To the girl who dream of meeting a prince
but end up falling for the misunderstood villain....

Preface

" The saddest thing ever is that
we both loved each other,
and then one day,
one fell out of love and
left the other still in love....."

♡♡♡

Acknowledgements

My sincere thanks to the people, for taking me ahead in the journey of writing this book.

My family members, for reviewing this book for the very first time and helping me with this work. My friends, for being the reader & for always keeping my spirits up and showing me the better way to bring this book up.

Finally, my greatest thanks to God, who is the first and last and all the things in between. I write for you, through you and only because of you. Thank you with my whole being....

And, You, the reader, holding this copy right now, my heartfelt gratitude for reading my work. I owe the success of the book to you....

Thank You..!!

ᗊᗊᗊ

Prologue

What can you say about a girl who lost her everything by the time the two of them were too close enough?

That, for whatever happened, she lost her faith in God? That she was incredibly in love with her boyfriend that, after he gone, she published her diary in his memory?

If we knew everything, everything !,right when we first meet people we would never fall in love. Can you imagine the weight of all of someone's secrets, insecurities, ex-lovers, questionable past behaviours, intimate scenes, their friends all on the first date?

Foreword

♡♡♡

.... **I Love You Abhi** ....

♡♡♡

Time and time again,
I forgave you...
Every time you hurt me.
But this time it's different,
You've hurt me one too many times,
And I don't know how much longer,
I can hold on.
My scars don't reflect,
How deep my cuts & wounds really are.
Nor do they show,
All the pain and suffering you have put me through...
The pain you gave me was unforgettable.
Then you destroyed me.
I'm standing here wondering what to do.
To start myself a new life.
Praying God will grant me someone to love,
Who will love me, like I had loved you .
As I write this.....
They're all for you.
Some may call me stupid and pathetic,
For loving someone like you.....
But what's the difference anyway ?
Because you've already torn me apart.
You've already ruined me,
But you're too blind to see that.
I am no longer the girl with the beautiful eyes
or beautiful smile,
I am now the girl drowning in her tears.

ϸϸϸ

1

Hi Shreya Singh (that's me)

I am finally putting pen to paper. I'm not sure if writing this to myself is the answer I'm looking for..

Let's see...

I am Shreya and I have been lying to myself for precisely one years now; the boy whom I loved, yet cannot marry.. But, as I have realized now, nothing lasts forever.

Now lying to others is fine, everyone does that. But lying to yourself !? That shit's hard, that will change you.. So Shreya, let's not lie any longer and let's say the truth, the hard truth and nothing else, and see if that helps us to survive...

There are many ways in which your life changes. Sometimes, changes happens slowly and sometimes it happens in a phone call, after which you can never go back to what was before....

I will never forget that day. I cannot forget that day. I can recall every single detail like it happened just yesterday, instead of one year back... That day defines me now. I hadn't seen him for many months before today. Life feels very empty right now. Everything had changed. " I don't think I knew I was lonely until I met you. When in love you tend to take each other for granted, and sometimes, that can cost you a lifetime of heartbreak and pain."

It was the darkest, sweetest of his memories. And the saddest of them all. The one which I repeatedly recalled for years, couldn't get rid of it. I couldn't live it with either. I smiled, wept, and burned at the same time, every single time it crossed my mind.

Not being with whom we want to be with, is such a pain that at least no doctor has a cure. Sometimes we put so many conditions on being with someone that it feels easier to be separated than to be together.

Life doesn't make sense anymore. It's said that life is a standstill when someone leaves; it's just a matter of habit.. One will get over it soon and so the other..

But is it so easy!?

Is it so easy to forget someone else the way you loved someone once and became unknown to him!?

Is it so easy that once you loved someone, marry someone else and leave the other alone in the most

crowded of places..!?

Someone once told me: 'You can't find yourself until you're lost.' Throughout my twenties, I never really understood what that meant. "You switch between cities, meet lots of new people, make homes out of strangers, and sometimes, watch them turn into strangers again."

There are always some people in our lives, no matter how badly they treat us, we always want to be with them. We cannot undo our feelings for them. We can't unlove them if we wish too.

We are all trying to survive someone's absence. So we keep lying to ourselves that we are okay without them. That's how life goes on, but deep down we know that it hurts. We keep on telling ourselves that better days await us but we know, deep down, the best days were the ones they spent with us. The days that were filled with echoes of laughter, silence and tears that were wiped with love. We are all trying to forget someone, someone whose memories make us a little more sadder than we should be. Love hurts, in unexpected ways. I moved in my life with his memories alive in my heart and keeping everyone aside in my head.

" Ah ! He broke up with me. He got what he wanted, actually he left for abroad, and he marry someone else." It wasn't the purest form of true love. He told me not to talk to him and all, everything finished in a fraction of time. To be frank, I would not say I have forgotten Abhinav, my love for him has grown since the day he left me and marry someone else !....... I still do but was it my fault ? Why wasn't I enough?

From being someone who loved him from the core of my heart, I now became the one who tried to avoid him at every step. From someone who waited the whole day to get a glance of his, I actually started hiding from him. Whenever I saw him with his wife, I would turn around and hide somewhere as I cannot accept the reality that I don't exist in his anymore. He even called me several times, but I tried to avoid him. How could I ? I felt cheated by him. I also felt a deep sadness within me. My friends and family members asked me the reason behind my sadness, but I didn't say anything.

" There can be a number of reasons why people leave you, but what they leave in you is something that can be left." How can my life have changed so drastically in less than a year? Yet it has, and it is a choice that he made..... Grief is easier to deal with. With heartbreak, the blame always shifts to you. You can put the blame on God, or destiny. It takes two person to build a relationship, but when it comes for break, one will put the blame to other without a shadow of doubt.

It's sad how sometimes we never speak to some people ever again. But we still remember them, their names will be one of the many things that never change, even if they decided to leave or even if they decided to hurt you. Sometimes we still remember them because we still have hope. We still think of them as the same, but people change, they do. And if they can't love us like the way they did the day before today, may be it's time to move on, may be it's time for you to put yourself first. I care. Maybe a little more than I should. And that's why it hurts. That's why eveyrthing bothers me the way it does. I feel too much. And I don't know when or how to stop it.

Since he left, I have learnt a lot about lust, love and life. Nothing is permanent, people changes, time changes and it changes everything around us - sometimes for the better and sometimes for the worse and no one can do anything about it. No matter how much we think we control our own lives and those of other around us, the fact is that we are not in control of anything. Without you, nothing is same. Everything hurts, but I need to hold on to these little echoes from the past, or I will go mad with your sudden absence. I never imagined my life without you, and I cannot accept the reality too. I thought I was yours forever and maybe I was mistaken.

I still smells like you, of the time when you were with me; embranced in your fragrance, I feel safe. It reminds me of the dreams we shared together, the warmth of the night we spent sleeping together. People have been telling me that I do not exist for you anymore, but I am not ready to go. Because you were the world to me, and I cannot bear the thought that I do not exist in yours and it hurts.

We should not forgot to express our love, ever! In our last few months together, I took you for granted. I took what was between us for granted as I never knew that all could be lost in the blink of eye. The few times when I did tell you how much I loved you, but you failed to stand by it. I should have told you more often how much you mean to me, I should have not hesitated in saying the three most sparingly used words in modern relationships. I never thought that you could go anywhere, that I could lose you. When in love, one should tell their beloved how they feel about them, how much they love them, how much they care for you. But, I realize that I was nothing, you are not there with me, not even then and not even now.

Life is moving forward for everybody around me, but I am exactly where you left me, for I do not want to move on. Everytime, I think of you, I close my eyes and go back, I feel you next to me. Everything reminds me of you. As soon as I wake up, I check my phone, hoping there's a message from you. But all is in vain. All I remember is you - us and your mistakes. I wish you could come back to me, talk to me, tell me how your day has been and ask me about mine. I want to hear you tell me how much you missed me all day; I wish to kiss your forehead once again. I would do anything to listen to you, laugh once again. I remind of those days - the world before we started fighting, the world before you started ignoring me for someone else, the world before you stopped saying, ' I love you', the world before ego crawled between us, the world before you leave me.

It was not easy to forget the moments that I had with you. It was not easy to forget the places where we had gone together. I never forget you. Never did your thoughts leave my mind. I can't even think of it. Each day it was getting more and more difficult for me and live without you. I tried to forget each and every thing between us but it never happened. I really missed you all day. I wanted to call you. But I controlled myself. I still remembered your message which said forget me and forget my name. But too be frank, I can't forget the pain that you gave me. I can't forget the days when I needed you the most and I was alone. I can't forget the time when I fought with myself alone.

Everything had changed. My life style had changed. My likes and dislikes had changed, I almost stopped talking with family members and friends too. I never wanted to curse Abhi. But I did. I cursed him, his life and everything. I feel bad about it

If I think practically I was taking my life to that end of the road. I, usually use to say:

No. I don't care. I don't love him. I don't want to see his face again. I am happy. I am enjoying my life. Who says my heart is broken? Am I falling for him? Who says?

Nevertheless, the fact was that I was just fooling myself by saying all this, as I always loved him, cared for him and will do it forever.

ppp

;)

"There was before you and there was after you. For some reason, I never thought there would be an after you. But there was, and I was in it.. Maybe I'll be in it forever...." ~ Anonymous

~ ~

2

Abhinav

On a pleasant February morning, I was, as usual, on my way to the office and get stuck on traffic jam. Suddenly, I noticed an old woman was trying to cross the road but she couldn't. At that time a young boy, on a bike, stopped and helped the woman to cross the road. The boy seemed very ordinary and polite. He was in a red t- shirt and a pair of blue denims, looked every bit as a Punjabi guy - light brown complexion, moderate height, short hair, trimmed light beard, a smart watch on his left hand and a sweet smile on his elegant face.

The cab moved alongwith the green signal of traffic but the greatness and smile of the guy left behind was just flashing back in my mind and heart.

I reached my office and breathed a little longer, went back to my desk & prepare myself for the day, but that boy..... That damn boy's feeling get stug in my head. I checked my emails and was almost through with my day's work within a couple of hours. My mind was recollecting the morning time. My thought flow was disturbed by the loud noises I heard from the corner of the room. I put my head up to see what was happening. I looked at him. My heart skipped a beat.

" Ah ! It was the boy..." The boy whose feelings had brought a storm of love to my heart, is infront of me....

I couldn't believe my eyes. Was it a dream; yet the conversation with the peon reveal that he was a new-comer employee. This is just unbelievable. I was on the top of the world. The HR introduced me with him and asked me to explain him the entire office work. He sat on the chair next to me. I was just speechless. I felt very nervous as the one I was thinking of for so long, feel an incomprehensive feeling next to me.

Adding to his charm were his smile with which he said " *Hi, I am Abhinav !*"

" *And I am Shreya* "

Our conversation began formally but, in no time, it became quite relaxed and informal when we found out some amusing things. " I learnt that he was born in the month of May and so am I..."

That was my first ever candid talk with a boy, whom I know just few hours ago. We touched base on various thing : the latest movies we have seen, our best friends, his family, my family, music and other area of interest.

Time passes by....

' *Okay ! I am leaving now. It was really nice talking to you Abhinav. But we won't able to talk more, though I want to...*'

' *Same here. I liked talking to you very much.... See you..*"

I left. I had really started loving him. I was continuously thinking of him. The feeling of him. The feeling of love. The feeling of romance. The feeling of being together. The day I met him I fell into his trap, I had lost.

That night, lying on bed, I went over the conversation again and again. And I wondered : "*Was he thinking about the conversation too, at that very moment, sitting somewhere in his room.*"

Alone in my room, I was smiling, talking to nobody and there was this different sort of feeling within me. I slept, just so that the night would pass, and a new day would come when I could hear his beautiful voice once again.

The next day, as I entered the office, I was surprised seeing him already sitting on the chair next to me. He said, " Goodmorning " and I too wished him....

ⲭⲭⲭ

<3

"Some people make the world special just by being in it." ...

3
The Meeting

We, usually, used to met in office. But this time we plan to met outside. The next day, we met for lunch. I had been excited the entire morning and had been looking forward to see him. It was quite late in the afternoon. When I met him, I felt he was too eager to see me.

The lunch we had that afternoon was extraordinary. We both had been eagerly waiting for this lunch since we were close. But that day onwards, I accepted that I was no longer the same I used to be. I accepted that I love Abhi's company. I got all excited when I was to see him at lunch. Our conversation went long and we share the most beautiful moment.

"Btw you're looking beautiful in this dress."

Hearing this I looked back at him and couldn't help myself from smiling.

To which I replied, "Thank you."

"Shreya have you ever fallen in love?" He asked me.

"No"

"You also never liked any one"

"I liked many. But I never loved anyone. May be I never found anyone who could be perfect for me. What about you?"

"Yes, I had been in a relationship for a year."

"So are you over it now? or still...." I asked.

"I am out of it. "

We left for our respective homes and had the best time till date.

<3

It's never enough;

talking to him...

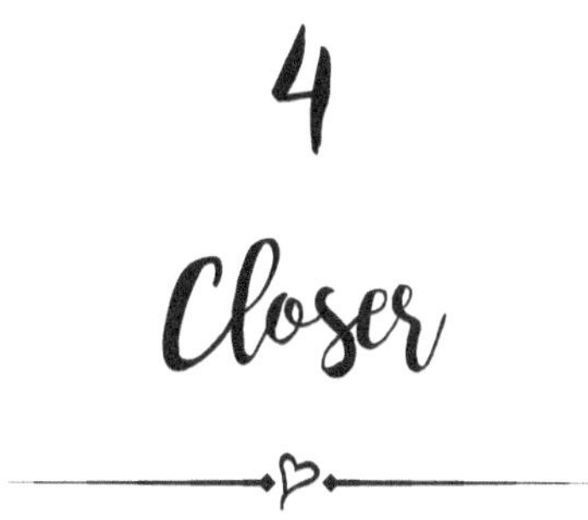

4

Closer

25th November, Wednesday. The day which was going to be remembered forever. The day I would get the world's best happiness. The day, which brings sunshine to my life. It was raining today. I really thanked God at that moment of my life, otherwise I wouldn't have met Abhinav.

1 message received. It was him only, my piece of heart.

Meet me in the cafe.

I replied.....

Okay! What are you wearing? Wear black, it suits you. What should I wear?

"Wear anything dear, you look beautiful in any colour."

The best possible and loveliest message at that moment.

I too wore a black dress and left for the café. Abhi was already at the cafe. I was a bit nervous.

"What do you want to say? Why have you brought me here Abhi?" I asked him as if I don't know what was happening.

"You know why you are here. Don't you?"

"Yes I know it. But I want to hear it from you."

My heartbeats were increasing continuously. I never had this feeling before.

19

He bend down on my knees, kept the rose in my hand and said the three most amazing word, I love you babe…. You are the love of my life. You are special to me. And every time I see you, I just want to hug you. I will never leave you alone in this relationship. Do you wish to be with me?

I had tears in my eyes. I had never that kind of feelings before. I nodded and said ….

I love you too Abhi.. Thanks for this moment. I accepted the rose and we both hugged each other.

We left the cafe, looking into each other's eyes. Everything was so beautiful. This is the memorable moment for my life.

I called him as soon as I reached home.

I went to my bedroom and relaxed on my bed.

It was a special day. I was not able to sleep. Whenever I close my eyes all the moment flashed in front of me. I had never experience this things before. Today I realized, what love was and why people used to say falling in love is always wonderful. This made my stomach full of butterflies.

❦❦❦

13th December. Sunday. We decided to go out somewhere. It was our first date. We did not plan it though. We were on a bike. I stood close to him. I put my hands on his shoulder. He blushed. I hold him tightly. I loved the moment. I did not care for the world. All I cared was for him. I felt special to him in my life.

"Love you"

"Love you too" I replied….

We reached and stop there for a while. He got closer to me. There was hardly any distance between our lips. We were both staring into each other. There was silence. Our relationship was moving so fast that after few days we were in a place so close that hardly any air passed between us. We were deeply in love. He was about to kiss me. I was breathing heavily. My heart began to beat faster, and the closer I got, the more nervous I became. He kissed me, leading to the most romantic moment, smiling between the perfect kiss. Our lips meet. Our first kiss last for more than a minute.. The kiss is what destroyed me. His lips are a weapon and when they touch mine, I become lost.

"Please don't leave me ever" I said, feared that he might leave me.

"No my love. I won't leave you. I cannot live without you. Love you.."

We went back. All that made me happy was that I had met Abhi. Nothing else was good. I enjoyed everything. I enjoyed the first kiss to my love....

:)

I want to belong to you..

Only you...

5

Us

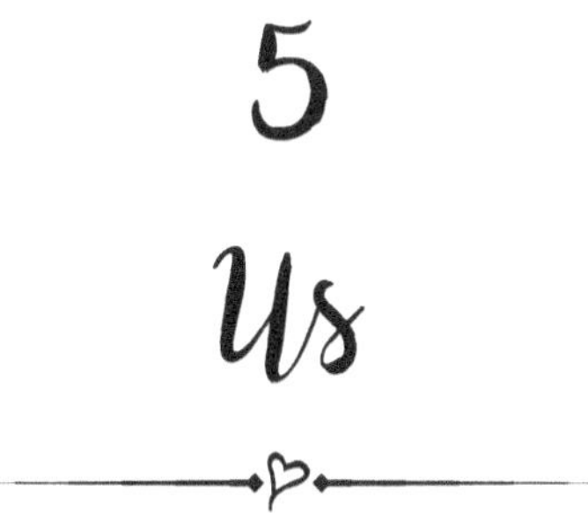

Encircled in his strong arms, I walks backwards slowly. Between his chin consumed by the desire because of the intoxicating fragrance of his body. His tongue draws the taste of my lips. I feels its softness on his lips and thinks how lucky I am to have him.

My eyes are half- closed. The touch of his tongue has aroused me. Abhinav nibbles at my skin and trembles with pleasure at the sweet pain. Pulling him between my legs, tightly clutching him. Abhinav holds me tightly, then holding the face in his palms he begins kissing my face all over. I melt in the warmth of his lips. I cannot bear it any more. He then pulls a little roughly into him even as we kiss passionately. His hands now slide inside my dress, feeling her, arousing her. He smiles to himself for having aroused like this. I moan, " Go on, ruin me. Wreck me please with your devastating love, Abhi..." He, then, runs his hand over the hook of my bra and opens it. I was breathing heavily. We stare into each other's eyes. I nod. He picks me up and carries me to the bed..........

ꠗꠗꠗ

.*
:

"Loved you yesterday, love you still, always have, always will." ...

6

Away From Him

Have you ever been alone - truly alone !

I remembered well. It was Thursday evening, around 4 p.m., I was on my way to home as I took leave from the office. On my way home, we were talking over text messages. I knew he would be waiting for my text and he really was. We'd decided earlier that this time we would be on chat. I was delighted to see him online. And so was he. But my delight was greater which is why I wrote so many messages...

"Hey... Babe... you there.

I have reached...

Where are you now? Office!?

Babe...

You there!?"

And he didn't reply, just asked me, *'Did you miss me?'*

"So much love. And you...?"

'A lot...'

And then we talked each other over phone. Hearing his voice after an entire day was so touching... We kept talking for a long time and then gave up, finally bade goodbye... Days passes by somehow. And our talks were for a short time over call and messages..

3rd March,

It was Monday... My third day at home. In the office, I used to met my colleagues and also with Abhi. But no matter I did at home, he was always on my mind. I missed him. Life wasn't too easy. We couldn't call each other whenever we wishes. We were on our chats and talk. Sometimes he replied within a second and sometimes it took an hour to get a single reply. But I can understand, this happens actually when one is running busy.

9th March,

We were on chat, just like any other day and I simply said; *"Babe, I love you and I miss you a lot. And I am really happy that you're mine.."*

To which he replied,"I am running busy... Please wait for a while. I was waiting all day long for his text but he was busy. I drop numerous messages and the last one I texted was *'Kab aaoge Abhi'*... I have to show you something..

After half and hour, I texted again..

"Are you online?"

I quickly got a replied ' *Yes love*',

'Where were you...?'

'Am so so sorry.. I made you wait for do long. Actually since morning, I am running so busy here and I completely forgot that you were online, waiting for me :('

'This happens sometimes' I replied.

'Btw I cannot wait for that thing you wanted to show me... Can you show that to me now?' -- He asked me.

And I replied, *'Yes... here comes those....'*

I gave him some pictures of mine... I didn't get a single reply even then...

I messaged him...

"Achii lag rahi hoon na main? Kuch kehna hain aapko!'

'*Bohot! This all are just beautiful...* I won't be able to explain you in words..'

"*Kissi ki bhi naa nazar naa lag jayee.*" And ....

And before he could complete his line his phone ranged and all he said was bye to me.....

20th *March,*

One morning - it was probably 10 o' clock - I was on my home and was going through my messages. Suddenly, I received a notification, and yes it was his message. As usual, he drop a message but this time it was something different. I opened the message. It was written -

"*Hey babe, going abroad for some work; will call you once I reached.*"

To which I replied, '*Please call me asap.. I am waiting for your call..*'

"*I am at the airport. You'll have to wait for a while.*"

Within next few hours, he called me. He told me that because of some work he been there and will come in a week. And listen, I love you. To which I moaned love you too.

30th *March,*

He boarded to India. On his return from abroad, my reliable boyfriend was acting more distant than usual. Now, this did worry me a little, but as I was in my home, I can't even express my feelings. He was a very friendly, caring but in those days he was very argumentative, which was unlike him. He had never been particularly emotional throughout our relationship, But I think I was emotional enough for both of us, no doubt.

I decided to call him and he picked up immediately. What happened then, changed my life forever. You know, one of the hardest things to admit is that we weren't loved when we needed it the most. "*The pain of not being loved, it's a terrible feeling.*"

'Hello'. I said *'Where are you?'*

He answered me *'Office!'*

'You didn't call me once. Is everything alright.'

'Naah.. Aisa kuch nahi hain.. I was running busy.'

In this year of relationship, he obviously thought I was stupid. I asked him why he being doing all these, but to be completely honest, he didn't respond to my questions . I was, literally, heartbroken. After a lot of screaming, shouting and tears from me, he disconnect the call. I honestly don't remember how or why he disconnect, whether I asked him to, or forced him to do this. In that moment of time, all I wanted him to do was tell me the truth. I didn't want to lose him.... I still wanted my perfect little family with this man. I called him again and again but he didn't responded. I cried.... and cried... and cried. I didn't think I had ever felt so alone; whenever I needed him the most he was never ever there for me but I accept him always the way he is but I truly hated Abhi at that point of time, it just seemed so unfair.

ᗡᗡᗡ

<3

<3

" *Sometimes good things fall apart so better things can fail together...*"

7
The Unexpected

'W-H-A-T ?' - Something stuck in my heart, I jumped off my bed,
" MARRIAGE ?" -- I rechecked.

'While he was in abroad, his family........'

My heartbeats increased.

" Yuvan, tell me the truth. What has happened? How this all happened."

He was silent.

'Speak up ! Goddammit.' I shouted at him. I could feel my feet shaking, losing their grip on ground. And I started rushing here and there in my room.

'I don't know, Shreya'

'What do you mean you don't know?'

He answered softly. ' One of my friend told me this about Abhinav.'

'Listen, I will call you soon to update you. Right now I have to go as the boss is calling.'

'Yeah..... yeah.... ya......You just go ahead with... I'll .... I'll wait for your call.'

I called Abhinav immediately.. He didnot pick up. I messaged him, he did not reply. I called him several times but there was no response.

After calling for several times, he received my call and without a pause he told me not to contact with him. He told me not to message him. It's too late..

'I love you so much.'

'Please don't get married.'

For months we had been dating, falling more and more in love everyday, but all he said was, It's too late..

'But Abhinav, we loved each other. How could you do that? I can't live without you. Do you flip a switch and erase me from your memory. The days when we were together means nothing....'

With pain, because of his happiness all I said goodbye forever to the love of my life.

But he didn't answered. And just disconnect the call...

I keep trying and trying but all was in vain.

Back in my room, I was still in shock, wondering if all that was real or just a nightmare and that when I woke up I would find a call from Abhinav.

But, unfortunately, it was real.

I cried. And I cried hard. I think I had never cried like that ever before.

I felt suffocated. So many fears crowded my mind. I didn't know what to do, so I rushed to the other room, to my worship - place. With my hands joined, I said to God, " Please God, Please. Don't do this to me. How could he get married to someone, instead of me. I literally loved him from the core of my heart. Why this all happened? Do he ever loved me at all? How could he do that!?"

At that point of time, I can't do anything. I can't even talk to my friends or my family members. Abhi was very happy. I want him to be happy. Even if that means I have to be miserable.

He was gone, leaving behind a part of him with me no one owned except me—and taking a part of me with barely anything. But it was over. Nothing could be shaped now. I knew he was gone....

Everything was over. I went back in my bed room. I closed the door.

I send him a message...... Message which communicated the end of everthing.........

"It's okay. Forget me. Forget my memories. Forget the moents I spend with you. Forget my name. Forget my touch. Forget the time we kissed. Loved each other or maybe I can say pretended to love each other. Forget each day we spend together. Forget my face. Forget my number. Delete it from my phone. Stay happily with her. I will never come along your way. The chapter of yours had been deleted from my life. I will always love you. I will always miss you. Yours and only yours, But you were never mine.....*

Whatever the reason is it was enough for me to conclude that this is the only thing left behind. It was not easy for me to send that message.. but I had to... No other option was left. I felt sad for myself . I was trapped. This was the sad end. I was ready to show I was okay with it. But somewhere it hurts. And it was the end of everything.....

ÞÞÞ

"And then you took it all away from me. You knew the whole time what you were doing, and how you were going to break me, and still you lured me back in."

8
The Present

---◦♡◦---

25th of November,

An unforgettable day. A special day. A day recalling him.

Another day arrives, so different from the exactly one year ago. This evening, I am recalling that day, when we met for the first time, when we talked for the first time, on the phone.

From someone, everyone & then no one - wanting to know - why I had to live like this. Had the second not put in appearance, I would have been married to him, celebrating the love. Had the first not put in appearance, there would have been no second one.

It was raining that day and it was raining today as well. I didn't have a love life then and I have none, now... I never thought that I would love someone the way I loved him and became unknown to him like this. That day, he was talking to me, questioning me, loving me, but he is not doing today I didn't know him at all then, he leave me all alone....

When I look back, I laugh and cry over those moments. Should I celebrate that once I had loved him or should I weep that he marry someone else. Look what I had once, and what I lost.....

Here, I am feeling so alone even in the most crowded of places, so much grief, so much pain.. Even the tears dried up.. But still, I have to live and I have to laugh..

Whenever I recall those moments, I just wonder, "Why I met Abhi ?' Lying on my bed, I wonder..... If I were in his place and he is mine, would he been able to survive without me ? Would he still have faith in God, which I lost long back ? Would he watched me marry someone else?......

I still can't understand how one can forgot true love, how one can forgot the one with whom they want to be with together. I was trying hard to forget it. But couldn't.

Today I think if I didn't met you, I would not have liked you. If I had not liked you, I would not have loved you. If I would not have loved you, I would not have missed you. But I did, I do and I will always. I can't talk to you anymore nor can I have you, but I can't help it because I am in love with you. There is this place where your kisses still lingers; where a part of you will forever be a part of me.

Why does someone love one person so much even if that person has betrayed her? I always gave it a thought. Still could not find an answer.

Six months later,

Things around me have returned to what they were some days ago, before Abhinav came into my life..... Without him, everything else have gone - my happiness, my dreams and many more... I have changed. It's been almost a year since I've laughed. But I have learnt to wear a fake smile. It's very difficult, but it makes my parents happier. When I am alone, I want company. When I am with friends, I want to be alone. Nothing comforts....

With the arrival of night and the passing of each day, I realized that another day of my life has gone. Some of my friends, have started saying me that I should move on and start a new relationship. But, how can I think of another relationship ? How can I think of another boy?...

" Exactly, Another Boy...!! "

What would I tell him ? That I spent the best day of my life with a boy who is not you? That I may have married you but I am still in love with a boy who marry someone else... That whatever you do, even when you kiss me, I remembered of him..... I keep asking myself these questions. And just because I don't have any answers, I remain speechless.

I stay isolated with people around me, as I can't bear the thought of leaving me. I turn speechless when people ask me if I miss him , would they understand that losing someone close is like losing a pebble, found walking down the street. Would they understand that I'm so used to people leaving me after being too close to me? It's not that I don't love him or care for him. But he was the one who decided to leave from my life like many others.

Stab my heart a thousand times and in the end it won't pain. I would just smile, wash my wounds and get ready for another dagger in my chest. That's what people used to. That's what life taught me. And I don't know if it's my fault. I think, at some point in our life, we all come to a point where we stop at such moment, where we wish we could either start over, or fast forward to the end in one go. If we could start over, once again, we do it in a heartbeat and maybe never repeat the same mistakes ever again. And if we could fast forward to the end, we wouldn't waste a second in doing that, because how gleeful it must be, to be able to escape from everything, that seems so eager to hold you down forever.

As I rub my eyes dry I take a deep breath look up into the clouds hoping for a day where my mind isn't crashing into thoughts of you. But I know that it's a fallacy. You are all I ever think about when I'm alone.

ÞÞÞ

I am at some place. I don't know exactly where. It's quite strange place. It is all bright around me. I don't know why I am here or where I need to go or what I want to do. The world blurs but I am walking. Though I never been to this before, but....

That scent..! I know that scent!

That scent reminds me of Abhinav. Everything glitters, I hear someone's heartbeat. All of a sudden I see someone in front of me. A boy! He is facing away from me. I am few steps away from him now. A cool breeze blows and everything around me changes. . I just can't move but stares at him; a tear from the corner of my eye rolls down. I want to speak but I can't.

I thought of how I seemed to have felt a strange connectionwith him. I thought of my past. I thought of Abhinav. The thoughts blurs my eyes. And all of a sudden everything went numb.

He vanishes.

My heart is still beating.

You're still okay by breaking me apart.

And I still love you......

:(

ᗡᗡᗡ

One years have passed by since that day. I was broken, broken into pieces.

Seeing the pictures of Abhinav & Deepika, I can't do anything instead I can only smile.

Confused, Sad or Happy? Even more confused.

Life would eventually find other ways to separate us - soon after his marriage I lose myself.

We're still not strangers I know him but we can never be what we once were.

What we could have been.

And yet, I still find solace in his smile because that was what I'd always wanted for him --- to be happy.

And, yes, how can I forget to mention:

"I wanna smile again..."

ᗡᗡᗡ

ᛣᛣᛣ

Last Night,
I put my ear against my back,
and listened to the rhythm of your heartbeat.
I slid my cold feet through your warm legs,
then I smelled the perfume of your neck.
Then, suddenly,
my body is shaken with pain and regret;
When I open my eyes just to see myself in bed.....
Alone...
Without You...!!

ᛣᛣᛣ

<3

ᗷᗷᗷ

Moral :~
   "Watching you walk out of my life does not make me bitter or cynical about love. But rather makes me realize that if I wanted so much to be with the wrong person, how beautiful it will be when the right person comes along."

ᗷᗷᗷ

People usually used to say, "If it's not forever, it's not love." But after all, forever is a lie.
True that.....

.